Three Lost Souls

Stories about race, class and loneliness

Woody Lewis

Gotham Lane

Three Lost Souls

Stories about race, class and loneliness

Published by Gotham Lane,
an imprint and trademark of
WL Solutions LLC.

Paperback ISBN: 9780997432817

www.gothamlane.com

Contents

Introduction

In his essay "The Talented Tenth," W.E.B. Du Bois called on the best and brightest African-Americans to distinguish themselves "from the contamination and death of the Worst, in their own and other races." He encouraged separation from the lower elements of black society, but in the second half of the twentieth century, some of the Tenth's descendants distinguished themselves by disavowing their race entirely. These were not tortured souls who passed for white, but social climbers who *acted* white to improve their chances. For this group of men and women, the road to assimilation ended in purgatory: they were conditionally accepted by the white race as they turned away from their own. We call them the Tormented Tenth.

Du Bois died in 1963, several months before JFK's assassination. While the social climate had improved, encouraging African-Americans to celebrate their race, some members of the Tormented Tenth apparently believed that the more you acted white, the better your chances were of fitting in, particularly in the Northeast. If you were smart enough, you could be admitted to an Ivy League college or one of the Seven Sisters, graduate with discreet fanfare and land a job that paid your way into a white neighborhood. Your liberal white friends would accept you socially, sometimes sexually. You could embrace their culture while ignoring your own, but in reality your achievements in business and those sectors of academia and the arts that forgave this behavior would enhance the torment you failed to acknowledge, or even recognize.

Here are three stories about such torment. The first concerns an idealist masquerading as a rock musician. Next, we see a writer in Los Angeles, caught in the grasp of what passes for friendship in that town. Finally, an academician tries to sedate her personal demons with professional ambition.

Three lost souls: stories of race, class and loneliness. See if you recognize anyone.

The Moralist

This is about a weekend in the country, up near Woodstock, around the time of the original music festival. You would think that after all these years, the memory would have faded, but that is not the case. I can see every detail, plain as day, and the words, though few were spoken, remain as clear as yesterday's conversation.

My therapist wants me to confront my feelings about what happened that weekend. She says that I need to accept responsibility for my actions, but when I tell her that Julian and Sasha were the protagonists, and I was just a bystander, she says to dig deeper. I explain that they were depressed, and she says that does not excuse their behavior. With each telling of the story, I move closer to agreeing with her.

Julian's prep school roommate had asked us to play at his wedding. Our band, the Braghan Chiefs, had just finished a week at Max's Kansas City, playing to a packed house of Warhol followers and our own crowd from Columbia. A critic for the East Village Other had written that Sasha, our singer, was the female reincarnation of Rimbaud. We were about to sign a record deal.

That Friday, Julian picked me up at my apartment on 112th Street. He and Sasha had moved down to the Village after graduation, but I had stayed in the neighborhood, partly because the Cathedral of St. John the Divine was my refuge. Whenever I felt the world closing in, I would walk down the block and find a place in the nave to watch the sunlight animate the stained glass windows.

Sasha looked like a mannequin someone had thrown in the back of the car, her arms and legs splayed at odd angles, her face hidden under a tangle of hair. Julian handed me the keys. "You drive. We've had a rough night."

He said they had smoked opium because his father had threatened to disinherit him. Sasha came from a wealthy Sephardic family, bankers and lawyers, dealers in precious metals, but that wasn't good enough. Julian's grandfather had been a crony of J.P. Morgan. His family expected him to marry accordingly.

I got behind the wheel and we drove up Broadway into Harlem, stopping for a red light at 125th Street. A group of teenagers on the corner stared at us. They pointed at Julian's ponytail and made fun of his appearance - the upturned nose, the astringent mouth. I was used to this because my black classmates at Columbia had done the same thing, making fun of my long-haired friends, questioning my judgment for associating with them. They warned me not to trust white people and told stories about what it was like growing up in the South, where trusting the wrong person, white or black, could get you killed.

Growing up in Brooklyn, my biggest concern had been fitting in. My mother sent me out of the neighborhood to a predominantly Jewish school near the museum. I was the only black kid in my class. Until I was twelve, I thought "*meshugeneh schwartzer*" was a salutation. My therapist says this is why I'm still trying to fit in.

We took the West Side Highway out of town. Julian wanted to hear something quiet so I turned on the radio and found a classical station playing *Appalachian Spring*. The angular melodies evoked images of country neighbors raising a farmhouse, couples courting at a square dance. We listened to the music as the city gave way to the country, the landscape flashing by as we drove north. Somewhere along the way, I saw a place where thickets of hemlock and red maple huddled over a river, the afternoon light filtering through their branches. A girl galloped a horse along the opposite shore, her blonde hair in a braid that bounced with the animal's gait. I wanted to be over there with her, to ride up off the river bank and walk our horses through a meadow.

We passed through a series of small towns that were uniformly clean and unspectacular. Everything looked bland except for a place in one of those towns, a brick colonial church with a white cross on its steeple. The windows had white shutters that gleamed in the flawless sunlight, and I imagined walking out into that light with the girl from the river after our wedding.

Sasha woke up a short while later. She brushed her hair until it crackled, then pulled it into a ponytail. Crouched in the back seat, she looked like a cornered animal, her expression narrow and furtive as she opened a compact and applied red lipstick.

"How do you feel?" asked Julian.

"Like I need to rest, not play another gig," she said in a scratchy voice.

"Doug's an old friend. The Chiefs are my wedding present."

"I'm not a piece of property you can pass around."

"You're still upset."

"Your father thinks I'm a gold digger."

"He didn't say that."

"In so many words."

And so it went for half an hour, bursts of anger from Sasha, followed by Julian's attempts to placate her. This was not just about his family's disapproval. We had been rehearsing or playing in clubs almost every night for the past several months. The people from the record label never left us alone. They liked to mix business with pleasure, and I wasn't comfortable with how Julian and Sasha were handling it. There were too many things that had nothing to do with music, too many parties where the undercurrent of expectations made my skin crawl, and there was always a moment, a pause in the festivities, when some girl would smoke a joint and start taking off her clothes, and it became a standing joke to watch me leave the premises. If we were in the country and I had no way to get home, I'd walk around all night, staying far enough away from the house so I couldn't hear the noise. There were times when I did this on acid and imagined that I was the last survivor wandering the ruins of a planet destroyed by vengeful spirits. I never asked Julian and

Sasha how they negotiated those parties. The most Julian ever said was that I should relax and let them handle it. Sasha never talked about it.

We turned off the highway and went down a private road to find the future groom sunning himself on the front lawn of a brick mansion. Julian greeted him like a lost soul. "Doug, you son of a bitch. Someone finally got your number, and she's from a decent family. Is it Alice?"

"No, the younger one."

Doug had the raw-boned looks of a Kennedy, but his eyes were different, colder and meaner. He ran a hand through his hair and looked at Sasha. "Not bad," he said. "Not bad at all."

We brought in our instruments and overnight bags. Doug told us the house had been built by his grandfather during the Depression to provide work for the locals. He introduced us to Mrs. Callahan, a heavyset woman in a grey uniform who showed us through the front parlor. I started to follow the others up a staircase but she stopped me. "We've special quarters for you," she said, pointing to a door near the kitchen. "It's quite private. There's just me across the way."

I went down the hall and opened the door to a room furnished with a single bed, a chest of drawers, and a straight-backed chair. From the window, I could see the woods in back of the house. I thought of my mother working as a live-in when she came up from Virginia after the war. She would have slept in such a room, and kept the door locked against the advances of her employer. Perhaps Mrs. Callahan thought I needed the same protection.

The others stored their things upstairs and came back down for a drink in the parlor. Framed photographs of Doug's forebears stared down from the paneled walls, the men looking grey and humorless, the women surly and judgmental. Julian smiled at Doug. "Did you spend much time here as a child?"

"As little as possible. Grandfather was a cranky old bastard. Isn't that right, Mrs. Callahan?"

She crossed herself disapprovingly. "That's no way to speak of the dead, Master Douglas." Her face was creased and weatherbeaten like a sailor's, her domed forehead balanced by the weight of her prizefighter's jaw. She wore her hair pulled back in a bun that heightened her severe expression. I had no doubt that Mr. Callahan was dead, and that if she had had any children, they had moved away, out of reach.

We went into town for dinner, where two girls joined us at a tavern. They introduced themselves as Meredith and Nancy, home for the summer from Wellesley. We took a table in the back. The people at the neighboring tables were not pleased to see me. One couple got up and left, the wife staring straight ahead, the husband muttering under his breath.

Doug sat between the two girls, and Sasha sat directly across from them, chain-smoking and grinding out the red-stained butts in a pewter ashtray. At one point, Doug said, "Sasha, are you all right? You don't look like you're enjoying yourself."

"I'm here to entertain you. It doesn't matter if I have a good time. Right, Julian?"

"Sasha, please."

"I'd like to be an entertainer," said Meredith. "I love being the center of attention." She had dark hair and Episcopal features, an expression of entitlement, as if nothing could go wrong, or if it did, someone would make it right again.

Sasha just stared at her.

After dinner, we drove back to the house. Doug rode with the girls in their convertible. We kept losing them in the rearview mirror. At the house, Mrs. Callahan was nowhere to be seen, but she'd left clean glasses and a bucket of ice on a sideboard in the parlor. I made a drink and sank into an armchair. Someone passed me a joint. Julian found some old LPs and put on Billie Holiday.

Sasha sang along with "Good Morning Heartache," shaping the words like Edith Piaf. Her accent would have been comical if she hadn't sounded so sad. Through all this, we kept drinking. The last thing I remember is Doug and the two girls collapsing in a heap onto a sofa across the room.

Sometime later, I felt a strong grip on my arm. Mrs. Callahan had shaken me awake, and she stood over me in the darkened parlor. "Come ahead, young man. You can't sleep out here."

She had undone her hair and it now fell loosely over the front of her robe. In the dark, she looked softer, more feminine. She had even put on a dab of perfume. I rose from the chair and she caught me as I started to lose my balance. She guided me down the hall to my door and we stood in front of it.

In the silence, we heard voices upstairs, and then a muffled commotion. "The last night of freedom for Master Douglas," she chuckled. She let go of my arm and touched my face. Her calloused hand felt rough against my cheek. I flinched involuntarily. Before she could respond, we heard an awful scream. Someone ran down the hall above us and slammed a door.

Mrs. Callahan hurried to the stairs. She took them two at a time and I followed her to the second floor, where she pounded on a door and then opened it.

Sasha stood at the foot of a four-poster bed, holding a belt in one hand and a drink in the other. She had on Julian's shirt and nothing else.

Meredith lay spreadeagled on the bed completely naked, her wrists and ankles tied to the bedposts with brightly colored scarves, an angry welt blossoming on one of her thighs. Julian sat in a chair, shirtless and dazed, as if he couldn't quite grasp what had happened. Nancy was on the floor next to him, struggling into her clothes. Doug was not in the room.

Mrs. Callahan snatched the belt from Sasha. "What kind of monster are you?"

She went around the bed, untying the scarves as she scolded Meredith. "And you're a fine one, you little whore. Wouldn't your parents like to know about this?"

Julian said, "Leave her alone."

"I'll just see about Master Douglas," she said and left the room.

Sasha walked over to the window. She finished her drink and chewed the ice, making horrible cracking noises. Meredith got up from the bed and rubbed her wrists. She folded her arms across her breasts and stared at Sasha. "Why did you have to hurt me?"

"That's what it's like when you're the center of attention. You have to smile, even when it hurts. It's not easy walking into a room full of people, like an animal on a leash, an animal they can have whenever they want." She watched Meredith collecting her clothes.

"You don't know what real pain feels like."

Nancy got to her feet. "You won't get away with this," she said. "I'll call the police."

"And say what?" asked Julian.

"Just you wait."

Meredith finished dressing and they left the room. We heard their convertible spraying gravel as it sped down the driveway. Julian smiled and leaned back against the wall, his hair fanned out behind him, his chest glistening with sweat. He studied the ceiling as Sasha sat down next to him. She ran a hand through his hair and sang a wordless tune that sounded funereal.

I went to my room and sat by the window, watching dawn break through the darkness. Despite the ensuing light, everything looked bleak and unforgiving. I realized that Sasha, despite her wealth, was an outsider to these people. Julian had joked that she was an *arriviste*. She had put up with it when no one else was around, but with Doug and the others, the joke must have brought out the worst in her, and it was Meredith's hard luck to be within reach. Of course, Meredith would chalk the whole thing up to adventure, the way rich girls did in those days. There would be no reprisal, and certainly no complaint to the police. Mrs. Callahan would see to that.

Eventually, I fell across the bed and closed my eyes. I was dimly aware of the wedding preparations happening around me, the caterers pulling up in their trucks, the deliverymen bringing flowers and folding chairs, the extra help brought in to transform the dark house into a place of celebration. I slept on and off for several hours, then showered and visited the kitchen. Mrs. Callahan was all business, ordering people around like a drill sergeant. I was lucky to get coffee and a buttered roll.

After breakfast, I went into the woods with my guitar. I poked through the brush until I came to a clearing and saw a pond riddled with cattails and lily pads. Waterborne insects skipped over the filmy surface, tracing lazy arcs through the algae. The mustard-colored sky was low and heavy.

I sat on a rock and played a few chords, hoping to write a song, coming up empty. No thoughts, no images, not even a melody. I felt like crying, but couldn't do it. No tears, no release. Just a tightness in my throat that made it hard to swallow.

As I experience that tightness again, I understand why

my therapist wants me to confront my feelings about that weekend, to accept responsibility for my actions, or more accurately, my inaction. I was not in the bedroom with Sasha when she mistreated Meredith, but I saw the aftermath and did nothing. Sasha was sad, but she was also cruel. I had imagined rescuing her from that sadness, but the sight of her standing in front of that bed, drink in one hand, belt in the other, absolved me of any fantasy. There was nothing I could have done for her. I realize that now.

Back at the house, our drummer and bass player arrived in their van. I helped unload the rest of our equipment and we carried it onto a stage that had been set up on the front lawn. Julian and Sasha came out to join us for sound check.

As the guests began to arrive, the Chiefs took the last row of seats facing a white gazebo on the south side of the house. We were halfway up a small rise that over-looked an expanse of wooded valley, a rolling carpet of green pierced by an occasional dormered roof. In front of the gazebo, a string quartet played Haydn and Mozart. Uniformed valets directed the arriving traffic onto a field past the end of the driveway. Those who could not, or would not walk up to the house rode golf carts that had been trucked in for the occasion.

A limousine pulled up in front of the gazebo. Just as the bride got out, someone near the house released a pair of doves. The birds chased each other from tree to tree, then settled on the roof of the gazebo, where they preened and fussed to the amusement of the guests.

The bride's father escorted her to the altar. They stood there for a moment, talking privately, and then he left her alone. She looked around, smiling tentatively, worrying the hem of her wedding dress. Sasha rose from her seat to get a better view. Julian looked bored by the entire proceeding.

A few minutes later, Doug walked out of the house behind a priest. They skirted the edge of the crowd, stopping at the first row to chat with a dark unsmiling man in his sixties who must have been Doug's father. He shook hands with the clergyman, who accepted a small envelope and hurried to catch up with Doug.

The couple turned to face the audience and Doug spotted us in the back row. He stared at Sasha until the priest spoke his name. The ceremony was short and to the point. Man and wife left the altar to the accompaniment of Pachelbel. The bar opened and the Chiefs took the stage.

We began our set with an arrangement of "Greensleeves," which Sasha sang in a distant voice, enunciating each word like a prayer. Doug took his wife to a square of parquet that had been laid out in front of the stage. The crowd applauded as the newlyweds waltzed. At the end of the song, Sasha continued with the wordless tune she had sung to Julian in the bedroom. Her voice grew fainter as the wind carried it over the trees. The last note died away, and in the silence that followed we heard the doves shuffling in the gazebo.

At the River's Edge

That morning, Jack called to say Arlene had hit it pretty hard the night before. Dinner was still on, she just needed to push it back a little. That was fine with me. I had fifteen hundred words due by five o'clock. Some south county rag you wouldn't use to wrap fish, but they paid well and I needed the money.

The piece wrote itself and I opened a bottle of Stoli to celebrate. I had a double on the rocks, put the bottle in a paper bag and left my apartment in Los Feliz. Anything to get out of that place. I would have moved out years ago, but I was watching *Double Indemnity* with Mary Alice one night when she said my building was the one Fred MacMurray's character had lived in, so how could I leave a piece of Hollywood history? She'd come over to tell me she was going to marry that two-bit lawyer and move to Palos Verdes. I wonder if she ever showed him my picture. Probably not. Why advertise a black ex-husband?

Jack and Arlene lived in an unincorporated area just outside of Burbank. Their house was at the top of a hill, and their driveway curved steeply as you came up from the street. They were proud of that place. Jack had scrimped and saved for years. He built movie sets for a living, steady work thanks to the union. They even paid to dry him out after that business down in La Verne. Took three months, but Arlene stood by him, just like the song.

It was still light outside when I pulled up behind Arlene's Mercedes. Jack kept his old Toyota down on the street so he wouldn't wake her when he left for work in the morning.

Arlene stood at the top of the stairs, posing in a low-cut halter and shorts that showed off her shapely legs, her face flush from the first Santa Ana winds of the season. With her porcelain complexion and baby's breath hair, she looked like a china doll with a low-grade fever, eyes bugging like two blue aggies. She had a thin, cruel mouth but could win you over with a smile whenever she wanted.

"You, Preston. Where've you been?"

"Busy," I said. "What's it to you?"

"My ass. Call a girl sometime."

"Where's your old man?"

"Out back. What's in the bag?"

I gave it to her and she pulled out the Stoli.

"All right," she said. "The good stuff."

I followed her into the house. She put the vodka on the kitchen counter and took a lime from a bowl of fruit. The counter separated the kitchen from a large living room. There were posters on the walls, mostly from Jack's movies.

Jack came in with a handful of tomatoes. "Just look at these babies, ripe as anything."

"Farmer John," I said.

He dropped the tomatoes in the sink and we hugged. We were the same height, six one, but he was twenty pounds heavier. He had broad shoulders and a barrel chest that felt like iron as he squeezed the breath out of me. His face told the story, the dull sheen from decades of hard drinking, the spider-veined nose broken playing high school football back in Milwaukee. And the eyes. My God, those basset hound eyes, peering out from under his tangled black hair, raging with pain and sorrow.

Arlene handed me a vodka tonic and made herself a Jim Beam on the rocks. "Cheers," she said. "It's good to see you."

Jack licked his lips. He went to the refrigerator, opened a bottle of club soda and took a long swig.

I saw four place settings at the table. "Who is it this time?" I asked.

Arlene swirled the ice in her glass and it made that tinkling sound you associate with gaiety and laughter.

"Dora's good people. We know her from church."

She took her drink to the bedroom while Jack turned on the ball game.

"What's Dora look like?" I asked.

"Not bad," he said. "Late forties."

"Divorced?"

"Almost."

I wanted to know more but the Dodgers were at bat. Jack was a man of few words, and fewer diversions. Baseball had always been important to him.

Half a lifetime had gone by since we'd met in New

York. Jack worked downtown but he lived on the Upper West Side near a bar that catered to Columbia students and the locals who tried to sleep with them. I spent more time in that place than I did in class, and Jack was one of the regulars. One night, Mary Alice walked in. Tall, dark and Irish, she'd just ditched her cokehead boyfriend because he'd been beating up on her. Jack offered to break the guy's leg, just to teach him a lesson. We bought her drinks until closing time and that's how it all started. The three of us wound up back at Jack's place. He passed out and I asked her to marry me.

The year before he moved out west, Jack lived with a waitress who kept a pet ferret. One night he reached for a glass of water and the ferret bit him on the hand. Jack waited until the waitress went to work, then took the ferret down to the river and set it free. When she came home that night, he said it wasn't right to keep an animal cooped up like that. She kicked him out, but the ferret was gone for good.

Arlene came back in a tight blouse and miniskirt. She had on too much makeup, but I didn't mind. The two of them didn't get out much and I knew she was happy to see me. Jack didn't care, but Arlene was twenty years younger. She wasn't used to staying in.

We finished our first round and she made another. Jack went through his bottle of club soda. It was nearly dark when we heard Dora pulling into the driveway. Jack went down to get her and I went to the window to watch.

Arlene came up behind me and put her arms around my waist. "When are we going to Palm Springs?" she asked.

"You're crazy."

"He's on location in Vancouver next month. We could spend the weekend."

I pulled free. "You know I can't."

"Why not?" She stepped back and vamped like a swimsuit model. "What kind of man says no to this? Why don't you finish what you started?"

I was about to answer when Dora entered.

"Is this a bad time?" she asked.

Arlene laughed. "Don't be silly."

Dora had on faded jeans, a sleeveless shirt that accentuated her muscular arms, and cowboy boots that added several inches to her height. She had the coiled presence of a predator, eyes darting around the room, looking for movement. Her skin was as brown as mine, and with her thick black hair and pre-Colombian face she looked as if she'd just come down from the mountains of southwest Mexico.

Jack came in behind her and if he noticed Arlene's agitation he didn't say anything. We all drifted into the living room. I got the feeling Dora knew what was up.

Her name was short for Isidora, last name Rodriguez. She belonged to the church Jack took Arlene to on Sundays and Thursdays, his idea of redemption. Arlene said the only reason she went along was because it reminded her of prayer meetings back home in Tennessee. She thought of herself as a good old girl, but in my mind she was too brittle for that distinction.

"I hear you're a writer," said Dora. "What do you write about?"

"Tender mercies."

"What?"

"Poverty, fourteen-year-old mothers."

"Any books?"

"None finished."

"Who's your favorite author?"

"Chinaski."

"Who?"

"That's what Bukowski called himself in his novels... Henry Chinaski."

She took a bottle of Bacardi from her bag and Arlene built her a rum and Coke. Then Dora and I went out to the patio while Jack said something to Arlene. He didn't sound too happy.

Outside, the Santa Ana winds had diminished. On a nearby hill, a stand of bleached yucca stirred in the moonlight. Dora studied the landscape as if expecting some amorphous presence to materialize in front of her. I asked about her husband and she spoke quietly, still looking off into the distance. His name was Tony and he'd left her for a younger woman who'd deserted him in Vegas. He'd come back begging Dora to forgive him but she'd refused.

"He runs off after twenty-five years of marriage and I should take him back?"

She fished a cigarette from her shirt pocket and struck a match. The flare illuminated her pug features. She had the face of a prizefighter, hardened by a look of despair her makeup failed to dispel.

"Was he rough to be with?" I asked.

She squinted at me through the smoke. "You writers are so observant."

Somewhere a dog howled, and the sound lingered until the other dogs in the neighborhood and the coyotes picked it up. I had more questions. Had she thought about a restraining order? Did she know there were agencies that handled cases like hers?

"Never mind my problem, what about yours?"

"If you don't want to talk about it."

"I mean Arlene. I see what's going on. She won't quit until she gets what she wants."

"She almost did, once. That's the problem."

"Then you need to cut bait, my friend. Throw this one back, there's tons more out there."

"You offering?"

She didn't answer.

"There you are," said Arlene when we came back in. She carried a tray of sandwiches, little squares with the crust cut off, the kind you make when you want to use up what's in the refrigerator and still impress your guests. Dora and I sat on the sofa and ate a few to be polite.

"Two of the nicest people I know," said Arlene. "We need pictures."

She went to get her camera and when she came back

Dora and I moved closer so she could get a nice shot. Dora flinched when I put my arm around her, but she managed to smile like a teenager. I felt her trembling and was egocentric enough to think it was my proximity. When Arlene had taken enough pictures I gave Dora more room and she seemed relieved.

I asked if she had any kids.

"Grown and gone. Son's in the Air Force, daughter married a ski instructor and moved to Colorado. I'm going to be a grandmother, any day now." She laughed, but then her voice hardened. "Wish I could share the joy with someone who'd appreciate it."

"We take what the Lord gives us," said Jack. "That's all we can do."

Arlene laughed. "You got that right."

Dora asked if I'd ever been married. I started to tell her about Mary Alice but Arlene rattled the dishes so loudly I had a hard time talking. Arlene had never met Mary Alice, but she resented the competition of her memory.

When we moved to L.A., the only work Mary Alice could find was waitressing. She tried the clubs on Sunset but the managers all wanted coke or a blow job, so she took what she could get: Denny's, Howard Johnson's; you name it. I was working on a screenplay, a remake of *The Defiant Ones*, the movie about two escaped convicts, one white and one black, but it wasn't the best time for a script like that. There was work in television if you had the stomach to write lovable black doctors with beautiful wives, or nerdy black teenagers wearing Pee Wee Herman suspenders and Coke-bottle glasses.

For awhile, we only had one car between us. If I had a late meeting and couldn't pick her up from work, Mary Alice would call Jack to give her a ride. I'd come home to find the two of them shit-faced on Bushmill's singing "Danny Boy" at the top of their lungs.

"Fucking Dodgers," said Jack. "Why bother?" He turned off the television and put on a Hank Williams CD.

I said, "Now you're talking."

Dora was surprised. "You like country and western?"

Jack laughed. "Preston thinks he's a good old boy. We ought to make him an honorary white man."

"What makes you think it'd be an honor?" I said.

We listened to a few songs, the usual litany of heartache, but Dora just stared at the floor. Jack sat next to her and offered consoling remarks. Once or twice, when she looked up at him, I saw a tenderness she hadn't shown me. I went to freshen my drink and Arlene tried to corner me in the kitchen. By this time, she'd put away a fair amount of Jim Beam. I retreated to the patio until she called us all to the table.

"Jack," said Dora, "how come you don't gain weight eating like this? I'd be as big as a horse."

"Arlene keeps me on my toes." He passed around a plate of pork chops. Dora took one and I took two, but Arlene just set the plate down. All she had was salad, and she hardly touched that.

"I can't believe you're going to be a grandmother," she

said to Dora.

"You and me both, honey. Now what about you two? When are you going to start a family?"

"Kids are too much work."

"How do you know? You haven't had any."

Arlene's eyes narrowed. "I know what it's like to raise a family," she said. "Poppa took off when I was twelve. Momma worked two jobs and went to night school to get her equivalency. I was the oldest, so I raised my four brothers and sisters. Cooked and cleaned, washed and ironed. No time for cheerleading, no time for boyfriends. Turned eighteen the day I graduated. Came home, fixed dinner, and waited up. Said, Momma now it's your turn. Took my Christmas Club money out the bank and caught the first Trailways headed west."

"How'd you meet Jack?"

"I was at Paramount for an audition. Saw Jack on the sound stage and we started talking. I didn't get the part but he took me to Spago's that night for dinner. I felt like a real actress walking into that place. We even saw Charlton Heston. I don't care what they say about him, he's a very nice man."

She sat down and raised her glass clumsily. "So here's to good old Jack."

The three of us clicked glasses.

"He really swept me off my feet."

Jack glared at her as she pounded the table for emphasis. "A real Casanova. What more could a girl want?"

Arlene got up to clear the dishes and Dora helped.

When they finished, we all went back into the living room. Jack turned on the television to find out the score and Arlene said it didn't matter, that the Dodgers were like him, born losers. He told her to shut up and she exploded.

"Don't tell me to shut up, you dry-mouth son of a bitch. What kind of a man won't even have a drink with his wife? That's right, just sit there with that hangdog look on your face. Can't even relax and have a good time without you looking over my goddamn shoulder."

She took her drink and stormed out onto the patio. We sat there, too stunned to speak, until Dora broke the silence. "Can a lady buy a cup of coffee around here?"

Jack looked relieved. "Coming right up."

"Make that two," I said.

We had our coffee and when Dora was about to leave Arlene came back in to say goodbye. "Thanks for coming over," she said as if nothing had happened.

Dora hugged her. "My pleasure, honey. You going to be all right?"

"Don't you worry about me. See you in church?"

"You bet."

I told Dora it was nice meeting her. We hugged and she followed Jack down to her car. He reached back to take her hand and they looked like an old married couple.

Arlene sat on the sofa and patted the place next to her. "Come over here and keep a girl company," she said, slurring heavily. I sat as far away as I could, but she moved closer until she had me wedged in. Her breath was shallow and medicinal, her lips wet with spittle. She tried to French-kiss me but I turned my head and she got my ear instead.

"Give me some sugar," she said. "What's the matter, are you afraid?"

She had her hand on my leg when Jack came back in.

"Leave him alone, you miserable cunt."

She got to her feet with difficulty and moved toward him. "What did you call me?"

He turned beet red and I thought, This is it. They'll kill each other and the cops will think I did it.

They stood no more than ten feet apart, both breathing heavily. I heard coyotes in the distance, yelping the way they do when they've cornered someone's pet. It's terrible to hear them tear an animal to pieces.

"Go to bed," said Jack.

Arlene sneered at him. "Make me."

He clenched his fists and started toward her, but she called his bluff and met him halfway. The fight went out of him and he slumped against a wall.

"I didn't think so," she said, stumbling past to the bedroom.

We heard the door slam and then she started pounding on it. She moaned and wailed and knocked things over like she'd been caged against her will. Gradually, the commotion subsided until there was no noise at all.

"I'm such a fool," he said. "Why can't I leave her?"

"You love her, I guess."

"I wish it'd been me instead of you who married Mary Alice."

"You made that clear."

"But you said it was all right."

"What I said was, wait until we're divorced."

Someone knocked loudly on the front door. It was Dora, looking very upset.

"Tony called me in the car," she said, "He's pretty drunk. Says he's waiting for me at the house." She looked around.

"Where's Arlene?"

"Passed out," said Jack. "Why don't I follow you in my car and teach that son of a bitch a lesson."

She went over to him. "Please, I'd rather stay here. Just for a while."

They started kissing as I closed the door behind me.

The Caregiver

He called out in his sleep. She went down the hall, said his name as she entered his room, hoping he'd know her, that he wouldn't call her a juju woman. He sat up, sheet twisted around his torso, his unseeing eyes darting back and forth. "Mattie?"

"I'm right here." She untwisted the sheet and freed him from it, his barrel chest heaving as if he had just run a mile. The heat of his skin. How many women would trade places, nightmares and all. "Do you want something?"

"Just stay a minute."

He held out his arms and she pulled him close, felt him shiver like a dog taken off a winter street. No words, just rocking back and forth. After a few minutes, he began to snore, his head heavy on her shoulder. She lowered him back down.

In the living room, she made another drink and went to the window. Traffic crawled up the West Side Highway, columns of red lights inching toward the bridge. She thought of the wives waiting for their husbands, the children for their fathers. Her own husband in the next room, haunted by the memory of his son.

She took the drink to her office and read the briefing paper again, this time making notes in the margin. *Simplistic. Inconsistent.* The author had called from Washington. He had dropped Pascal's name, but she suspected they were mere acquaintances. Mattie had not spoken with Pascal in months, but she knew that he despised mediocrity, that he would have dismissed the paper and its author.

In the morning, her husband stood in his pajama bottoms making breakfast, the sunlight illuminating his broad shoulders, eclipsing the dark spirits. She came up behind him and put her arms around him. "How do you feel?"

"Like he was in the room, Mattie. I heard his voice."

She felt his heart pounding. "Come back to bed."

"I'll be late," he said, pulling free.

He had been like that since the accident. She had heard about women grieving, losing interest, but not men in their prime. If she had been the jealous type, she might have suspected him of cheating. Over the years, she had gained a few pounds while he had remained at his playing weight. She wondered if men still found her attractive.

Walking up Riverside Drive, Mattie reviewed her commitments. She had buried herself in work, editing a manuscript, taking on administrative duties, an extra class. Had she not been preoccupied, the day might have enticed her. Warm breeze, brilliant sky. Couples in the park, kissing. She hurried across campus.

Her assistant had called in sick. Mattie was at the desk in the outer office, going through her mail, when a man knocked on the door.

"Doctor Prudhomme?" He was young enough to be a graduate student. Clear blue eyes, a thatch of sandy hair, an earnest expression. He had on a dark suit, white shirt and club tie. "Jack Crawford," he said. "We met last year at the confirmation hearing."

They went into her office and she waved him to a chair. "You were counsel to the Secretary-designate. Now, you're his chief of staff."

He nodded. "Then you know about the job?"

"I've heard talk."

"You're at the top of the list."

She turned to look out her window at the columned library, at the names on the entablature. Aristotle, Herodotus, Demosthenes. Guardians of truth.

"Why me?"

"You're an outsider. No history, no baggage."

"When I think about the Beltway, why anyone would choose that life."

"After a while, nothing else matters. Feels like I've been there forever."

"How long has it been?"

"Four administrations, counting this one."

She turned back to face him. "Wife, kids?"

"In Chicago, with a guy who comes home for dinner."

"You're divorced? That's hardly an endorsement."

He spoke carefully, his eyes searching hers. "I'm not here to spin the lifestyle. We're at a critical point and there's a lot to accomplish. The other side will hijack policy if they can. We need your expertise."

She had never seen such blue eyes.

"I'm comfortable here. Why should I leave?"

"Have dinner with me."

When she returned home that night, she heard the boy laughing. She closed the door behind her and listened as she walked down the hall to her husband's room. She knocked and entered, found him sitting on the bed watching a video. The boy looked exactly like him, except for his complexion: *café au lait* instead of obsidian.

"How was work?" she asked.

Her husband stared at the television. "He was five when this was taken."

The boy ran out of the frame, the camera following his mother as she hurried after him, her red skirt billowing like a sail.

"I asked how your day was."

"The same."

She closed the door and went to the kitchen, made a drink and started preparations for an *étouffée*. The boy's mother had given her the recipe. She had brought him up for the summer, had agreed to let him stay with Mattie and her husband, joking that she would put a curse on them if anything ever happened to him. Her face had darkened when she said this, a shadow passing over the features that would have been called *quadroon* in another time.

That summer, Mattie joined Pascal at the institute. She commuted to Princeton every day, wrote papers, did research. They traveled to conferences and plenary sessions, a blur of different cities, Pascal pushing himself to exhaustion, his face whiter than usual. While this was going on, her husband enrolled his son in baseball camp. He said the boy was a natural at first base, as he had been in college. The camp shot videos of every game.

Mattie finished her drink and made another. When the meal was nearly ready, she knocked on her husband's door again. Silence. She eased it open and found him asleep on the bed; next to his outstretched hand, an orange bottle of pills. She counted and found two missing, not enough to cause concern, just another night alone.

The following evening, Crawford met her at a bistro on Columbus Avenue. He had on the same suit, a shirt open at the collar, no tie. The shirt was cobalt blue, like his eyes.

Instead of sitting across from her, he took the seat to her right and she was comforted by his proximity. The waiter brought a bottle of her favorite bordeaux and Crawford smiled at her reaction.

She asked about his background, mostly to hear him talk. Born and raised in Duluth, undergraduate at Northwestern, law school at Chicago. "Is that where you met your wife?"

He shook his head and looked out at the street. She followed his gaze and saw a woman pushing a stroller past the window.

The waiter returned to take their order. *Coq au vin* for her, steak tartare for him. Mattie wrinkled her nose. "How can you stand raw meat?"

Crawford laughed, dispelling whatever the sight of the stroller had evoked. The pitch of his laughter, the adolescent sound of it, conjured the boy from Connecticut who had laughed the same way.

Mattie had fallen for that boy, who had also been sandy-haired and blue-eyed, in her sophomore year. She had not intended for it to happen. Her sorority sisters had warned her. *Girl, you must be crazy.* In the end, they were right. The boy moved on with no explanation. Mattie heard later that his family had threatened disinheritance if he continued seeing her.

Crawford continued his argument. "I've read your book, and the work you did for Doctor Chaminade. You'd be a tremendous asset to the Department. There's no one better suited for this position."

He was shrewd to mention Pascal. He knew that she would ask Pascal about the job.

Mattie studied Crawford as they ate. She imagined his ex-wife listening to him night after night, sharing his success, then tiring of it, the two of them separated by the gulf of his ambition.

The boy from Connecticut had been the same way, talking about his plans for a future Mattie never got to share. After the breakup, her sorority sisters introduced Mattie to their inner circle, family friends they had known since Jack and Jill. She went to the right parties, vacationed in the Vineyard, and met a succession of willful young men, bankers and lawyers who saw her as an appendage to their careers. She was light-skinned enough to attract the best prospects, but they acted as if they were doing her a favor, as if she were fortunate to be in their presence, and they found her tepid response offensive. There was talk of not knowing her place, not playing by the rules, but that only heightened her indifference.

She went on to graduate school, where she met her husband-to-be, who had turned down a minor league baseball contract to attend business school. Mattie appreciated his unassuming nature, the product of an impoverished childhood. Her sorority sisters tried to dissuade her, warned that if she had children by him, they would be too dark. She claimed not to care, but never told him what they said. It was only after they became engaged that he told Mattie about the boy in Baton Rouge. He told Mattie that the mother would raise the boy, that he would give her money. The arrangement sounded heartless to Mattie, but not enough to change her plans.

Her sorority sisters chided her for not being diligent. *We thought you knew.* They attended the wedding, polite to a fault, but Mattie knew they were jealous. She had married for love despite its encumbrances, a concept as foreign to them as her indifference to their ambitions.

Crawford's cellphone rang. "Excuse me," he said. "I need to take this." He went outside and stood near the window, his expression vacillating between concern and annoyance. When he returned to the table, he forced a smile. "Nine-year-olds weren't meant to fly," he said. "Not from trees, anyway."

"Is everything all right?"

"A few stitches and a bruised ego."

"She still calls you?"

"When it's serious."

He paused to look at her. "You've been through worse."

"That was a freak accident. The boy had no time to react. He couldn't get out of the way." She recited the facts like a catechism.

He took her hand. "What about you?"

"My husband has post-traumatic stress disorder. He saw the whole thing happen. I don't know if he'll ever be himself again. Thank God he found a job."

"He's not doing well."

"You're surveilling him?"

"I went to school with one of the partners."

"He just needs more time."

"They're about to let him go."

She knew nothing of this.

As they finished their meal, Crawford said that if she took the job, he would find something for her husband. He spoke with the conviction of a negotiator about to close a deal. Pascal had taught her to recognize the moment of truth, which she now saw as clearly as she had seen the accident. The boy at first base, crouched and ready, watching the batter swing, trying to avoid the ball coming at him, unable to raise his glove in time, the ball hitting him in the face, the boy dropping to the grass.

Her husband watched the video over and over until she took it away. The boy's mother sat by his hospital bed for two weeks, exhorting the spirits to disperse the coma that had engulfed him. Mattie's husband receded into his own darkness, unable or unwilling to respond when the doctors told him the boy's brain had died. In the end, it was Mattie who convinced the mother to give the order, to take the boy off life support.

The waiter brought dessert menus. Mattie shook her head. "There's one more thing," said Crawford. "I hope you don't mind my asking. Why did you continue traveling after your son's death?"

"Stepson. We have no children of our own."

"Why stay away when your husband needed you?"

"I was at a critical point in my research. We were about to receive more funding."

Her hand trembled as she reached for her glass. She looked up at Crawford. "You already know the answer."

"I'm sorry, but I had to ask."

Pascal had thought they were discreet. She should have known better, but the accident had overwhelmed her. He had offered affection and she had accepted. No one had been hurt. She did not think of it as a betrayal.

Crawford was tactful. "Doctor Chaminade looks forward to working with you again."

He called for the check as Mattie excused herself. She went to the ladies' room hoping for a good cry, but barely managed a tear. As she repaired her makeup, she remembered what Pascal had told her, that excellence had a price, that she would be lonely in her success.

She returned to see Crawford outside hailing a cab. A young family, a couple with a newborn and a toddler, had just entered the restaurant. The father held the baby in his arms while the mother fished around in her purse. The toddler cried for attention, arms outstretched, waiting to be picked up. Mattie hurried past to join Crawford in the cab.

About the Author

Woody Lewis has published work in *The Southampton Review, CONSEQUENCE magazine, Los Angeles Review of Books* and *Mashable*. He has worked as a rock musician, investment banker, graveyard shift security guard, jazz composer and software engineer - in that order. Born and raised in Brooklyn, he spent most of his adult life in northern and southern California, returning with his wife and son in 2010 to New York City, where he is at work on a memoir and a novel about Silicon Valley. He has a B.A. and M.B.A. from Columbia University, and an M.F.A. from the Bennington Writing Seminars.